# Winter Lullaby

Dianne White

illustrated by
Ramona Kaulitzki

CANDLEWICK PRESS

Cool winds blow through graying skies.
Geese are honking long goodbyes.
Autumn clouds sweep overhead.
Let's go, Small Bear. It's time for bed.

But, Mama, Mouse just scurried by.
If she's not sleeping, why must I?
And look! There's Chipmunk, wide awake,
gathering nuts beside the lake.

Mouse is rushing to her nest.
In soft, dry grasses she will rest.

Chipmunk stores his cache below
before he curls beneath the snow.

Look, Mama, two friends over there.
Skunk's waking up, and so is Hare.
See them romping round the trees
and tromping through the fallen leaves?

In just a while, deep underground,
Skunk will slumber, safe and sound.

Hare will weather winter's storm
in empty log or hollowed form.

Badger pauses in the light.
Where will she spend this frosty night?

And Old Raccoon—what will he do?
If he stays up, I'll stay up, too.

Badger will settle—soon, not yet—
tucked inside her chambered sett.

Raccoon will go back to the glen
and crawl into his cozy den.

But I don't want to go inside.
When winter comes, why must we hide?

As winter dims to charcoal grays,
bears sleep and wait for greener days.

And when spring comes, we'll both awake?

We'll splash together in the lake!

The world of ice will melt to green?

The days will brighten. First, to dream!

It's time, my cub, to close your eyes.
The night sings soothing lullabies.
We'll snuggle close all winter through.

I love you,
Mama.

I love you,
too.

To my great-nieces and great-nephews:
Benjamin, Annabelle, Adeline, Cora, RJ, and Raymond
DW

To Maximilian
R K

First edition 2021

Library of Congress Catalog Card Number pending
ISBN 978-1-5362-0919-8

21 22 23 24 25 26 CCP 10 9 8 7 6 5 4 3 2 1

Printed in Shenzhen, Guangdong, China

This book was typeset in Tienne and Junction.
The illustrations were created digitally.

Candlewick Press
99 Dover Street
Somerville, Massachusetts 02144

www.candlewick.com